Belle's Wedding Day

1

Belle will marry the Prince.

What will Mrs. Potts do?
She will make a dress.

What will the tailor do?
He will make a suit.

What will the florist do?
He will make a bouquet.

What will the chef do?
He will make a feast.

What will the musicians do?
They will make music.

What will Belle and the Prince do?
They will dance!